Charles Clement Walker

John Heminge and Henry Condell, Friends and Fellow-Actors

of

Shakespeare, and what the World Owes to them

Charles Clement Walker

John Heminge and Henry Condell, Friends and Fellow-Actors of
Shakespeare, and what the World Owes to them

ISBN/EAN: 9783744729109

Printed in Europe, USA, Canada, Australia, Japan

Cover: Foto ©Raphael Reischuk / pixelio.de

More available books at **www.hansebooks.com**

FRONT VIEW OF MONUMENT.

JOHN HEMINGE

AND

HENRY CONDELL

FRIENDS AND FELLOW-ACTORS
OF SHAKESPEARE

AND

WHAT THE WORLD OWES TO THEM

BY

CHARLES CLEMENT WALKER

1896

LIST OF ILLUSTRATIONS

PREFACE

THE following pages are a slight attempt to show the reasons that have actuated the writer to erect a monument to the memory of John Heminge and Henry Condell, the friends and fellow-actors of Shakespeare, who several years after his death collected and published his dramas in 1623 " according to the true original copies."

Without doubt a memorial to these men should have been raised by public subscription, but wide inquiry showed that while Shakespearian scholars well knew their merits and how much mankind owe to them, their names are almost unknown to the generality of readers ; and of their merits, not one in a thousand of English-speaking men was conscious. This has probably arisen in consequence of most of the editions of the Works of Shakespeare being without the Dedication and Preface signed by Heminge and Condell, which appeared in the First Folio of 1623 ; and in biographies of Shakespeare which may be attached to the later editions, these actors are simply alluded to as having published his plays, so that their names are almost unknown. But, as will be seen, what we owe to them is of such inestimable value that if

public monuments are to be erected to our public benefactors
none are more worthy to be commemorated than Heminge
and Condell, to whom alone the world is indebted for this
first edition of what it calls "Shakespeare." Their own story
of the reasons which moved them to publish this collection
is such a beautiful instance of unselfishness, singular love of
Shakespeare, and unaffected modesty, that the writer felt it
only needed to become well understood by the public for
their merits to be appreciated. The most certain way to
bring about this desirable result was to erect a monument to
Heminge and Condell to be before the public eye. The
writer hopes that this explanation will be counted a sufficient
apology for his attempt to do honour to the memory of these
two English worthies so long neglected.

It only remains for him to thank the Rev. C. C. Collins,
M.A., vicar of St. Mary the Virgin, Aldermanbury, for the
heartiness in which he assisted in the work, and for his
researches in the Registers and Parish books which have
enabled the statements made of their relations to the parish
to be verified. His thanks are also given to Dr. Furnivall,
the founder and director of the New Shakspere Society,
whose great and critical knowledge of all relating to the
Bard of Avon has been freely given when required.

FRONT TABLET.

JOHN HEMINGE and HENRY CONDELL
FRIENDS AND FELLOWS OF SHAKESPEARE

WHEN Lord Tennyson—the greatest British poet of this generation — was laid in his grave in Westminster Abbey, the Works of Shakespeare were placed by his side. While he lay on his death-bed, being unable to speak, he motioned to those about him to bring this volume ; and opening it, he pointed to words expressing the thoughts he wished to utter. His family regarded this volume, which had been his life's study, as too sacred to be any more used ; they therefore buried his treasured Shakespeare with him. Such an incident attracted public attention, and it was then stated that the Victorian Laureate always spoke of Shakespeare as the greatest of all poets ; and said that while he was able to form an idea of the intellectual efforts of other poets—their state of mind being comprehensible to him —of the state of mind and feeling that found expression in Shakespeare's dramas, he could form no conception whatever; and Shakespeare was the master at whose feet he was willing to sit.

It is now nearly three centuries since the volume we call "Shakespeare" appeared before the world. Age has

not dimmed its brightness ; Time has proved its pre-
eminence. There is probably no other masterpiece of
literature which in the circumstances of its evolution has
had a more remarkable history ; and for the possession of
this treasure we are indebted to two men well known to
Shakespearian scholars ; but by ninety-nine out of every
hundred persons of the present day who read Shakespeare
their names have never been heard of. They are John
Heminge and Henry Condell.

To those who have investigated all that is known of
the drama of that period, it has always appeared extraordinary that Shakespeare—one of the numerous family of
a plain tradesman, who, with his wife, could not write their
names—with his limited early education at Stratford-on-
Avon, and his subsequently active career, should have
produced such a remarkable set of compositions as his
dramas. Although much has been discovered by research
that was not known a century since, yet the wonder still
remains. This is the origin of those strange attempts
to father the poet's plays on Lord Bacon, notwithstanding the
testimony of the ablest actors—like Sir Henry Irving—that
none but an accomplished master of the stage could have
produced them, which Bacon was not. But while we are
unable fully to explain their production in such circumstances
as developed Shakespeare, we have no such difficulty in
showing to whom we are indebted for the preservation of
his writings. Yet although they are more extensively read
than ever, and the interesting spots in his native town
are visited by increasing numbers from all parts of the

BUST OF SHAKESPEARE

world, the names of these treasure-keepers are almost un-
known without reference to books, except, as stated, to
Shakespearian scholars,—who speak with all gratitude of
John Heminge and Henry Condell who both collected
Shakespeare's plays and gave them to the world, and thus
preserved them as a possession of mankind for ever.

The career of Shakespeare may be briefly narrated.
He was born in 1564. After going to the Grammar School
at Stratford he left at the usual early age, probably twelve,
to learn the business of his father, a glover, a dealer in wool
and woollen goods ; and probably a keeper of sheep for their
wool, for there was a tradition of Shakespeare being a
butcher. He married Ann Hathaway very early—who was
eight years his senior ; his first child was born before he was
nineteen, and before he was twenty-one he was father of
three children. From all that is known, he seems to have
been compelled to leave Stratford, and went to London. His
father was enterprising, and had been well-to-do, but his
affairs were then getting into a state of insolvency. It is
supposed Shakespeare obtained a situation at "the Theatre"
in Shoreditch, the first and only one in England, built by
John Burbage, a carpenter, one of a company of players.
It is not known that Shakespeare was ever engaged in
theatricals before he went to London. In about seven years
after, we hear of him in 1592, as being then both an actor and
writer of plays. Blank verse had been recently introduced,
and was successfully employed by Marlowe, a dramatist. The
plays were mostly written by University men, who were very
dissolute, not to be depended upon, and who wrote to obtain

B

money for their necessities. Almost all died at an early age
through their excesses. Shakespeare, we know by subsequent testimony, was "a deserving man," and while learning
to become an actor, practised writing, after the best ex-
amples, and doubtless was useful in furnishing prologues and
epilogues to other plays to give them novelty; thus, feeling
his way, he had when he was twenty-eight years of age
produced at least one play. To have done this in seven
years is proof of his industry and ability. It was a great
advantage to have such a person in the theatre, for he was
always at hand, and to be depended upon, while the playwrights were recovering from their debaucheries. His life
was now most active, he was continually playing, dressing
up other plays, or it may be—as many did in the pressure
of producing them—working with two or three others in
getting a new play against a rival house. There is a record
of six writers working in the production of one drama.
This necessitated great speed in composition. By 1598
he had become a shareholder in the theatre, and had
produced several of his well-known dramas, and was admired
for his poems of "Venus and Adonis" and "Lucrece." We
know that he was then associated with Richard Burbage (son
of John Burbage), Heminge and Condell; and in a year
or two after the whole company removed to Southwark
to a new theatre which they built, and called the Globe;
and there he continued till he closed his connection with
the stage about 1612, and left to spend his days in retire-
ment at Stratford, having acquired a moderate fortune, while
most of his fellows and friends continued their profession.

BUST OF SHAKESPEARE

It is well to try to realise the life that Shakespeare lived during these years. While playing regularly at their theatre during its season in the daytime, actors were in demand for pleasure elsewhere at nights, playing at great men's houses, or in yards of inns, and in summer, travelling as a company in various parts of the country; and except they were licensed under the protection of a nobleman as his "company of players," as some were, actors were looked upon as little better than vagabonds. Indeed, in the City of London they were not permitted to play at all, so they had their theatre outside the walls, at Shoreditch, and afterwards in Southwark across the Thames. Shakespeare never brought his family to live with him in London. He always lived in lodgings, and usually near the theatre. He went down to Stratford, where his wife and family were, away from all the discreditable scenes surrounding the theatre, bought property there with his earnings, and saw his children well provided for, and brought his father and mother out of their pecuniary difficulties, while he himself returned to London, playing there both by day and by night, and in his scanty leisure, producing two or three dramas at least each year, often under the most pressing circumstances, and with a speed that astonished his fellows, accustomed as they were to hasty productions. Queen Elizabeth having seen Falstaff in *Henry IV.*, greatly enjoyed it, and expressed a wish that she could see him in love. She was soon gratified, for Shakespeare produced his *Merry Wives of Windsor* in a fortnight. The public demanded a continuous succession of plays, usually a fresh play every day, for no plays had long "runs" like some of the present day. There were numerous playwrights; Shakespeare was but one of many. He, like others, had to play in many pieces written by other men. New dramas were necessary. We know that one on an average was produced every seventeen days. The parts had to be learned, they had to be rehearsed, other duties of the theatre had to be performed, and when plays were stopped by public order in London on account of the plague, then so prevalent, the actors had to travel the country, setting up their booths in inn-yards, knocking at great men's doors in seasons of festivity for permission to play, applying for temporary licences to act from the local magistracy (often refused) putting up with any accommodation they could get at inns, and frequently disturbed with the roar of the customers. While it was a real pleasure to them to play before the Queen at Greenwich, and be appreciated by her, their principal occupation was to please the public. Under all these irregular, disturbing circumstances, our truly admirable national poet produced those thirty-six splendid dramas, which are our country's pride; and when all is considered they must be pronounced marvellous productions.

Shakespeare probably sold all his interest in the theatres, and retired from his active life at forty-eight years of age, to live on his hardly-acquired property in quietness in his native town, but he died four years afterwards, in 1616.

There is no sign whatever that Shakespeare contemplated the publication of his dramas. He of necessity must have been well aware of their superiority to those of his compeers. Several had been published, taken down in some cases by shorthand writers while hearing their performance, or surreptitiously obtained from the acting parts. They were valuable property of the theatre that owned them, and their publication would have enabled rival theatres to play them ; so the owners used all possible means to prevent it. Indeed an attempt in the year 1600 to publish *As You Like It* was frustrated by an appeal to the Stationers' Company. Only very few of those printed had been revised. The book-sellers made an arrangement with the Company of the Globe Theatre who owned them, to obtain the sanction of the Master of the Revels (who had the duties of the present Lord Chamberlain, but with more power) for the publication of *King Lear*, played before King James at Christmas 1606, and it ran through two editions at once. Plays were looked upon as written to be spoken ; and nothing but what was very popular, as likely to sell, was even surreptitiously got for printing. J. P. Collier who made so much research, supposed that fifty times as many plays had perished as were printed. It is quite certain that most of those which remain, rare as they are, have been recovered and preserved, chiefly by reason of the great research into the drama of the time, through the over-whelming interest taken in everything likely to have had influence on so unparalleled a phenomenon as Shakespeare.[1]

[1] So rare are these quartos, as they are called, that while a fairly perfect First Folio will fetch at least £800 to £1,000, these command a much higher relative price. Within the last six years the following prices of some have been realised by auction : *King Lear*, £100 ; *Henry V.*, £145 ; *Midsummer Night's Dream*, £122 ; *Merchant of Venice*, £146 ; *Romeo and Juliet* (a fourth edition), £107 ; *Love's Labour's Lost*, £140 ; *Merchant of Venice*, £270 : *Much Ado About Nothing*, £130, and a small volume entitled *Sir J. Falstaff and Merry Wives of Windsor*, first edition, was sold for £385. *Hamlet*, a

Up to the time of his death, there had been no collection of dramas printed of any dramatist. The great speeches of the orators of former ages that electrified their hearers have nearly all perished ; and while this is so with burning thoughts on absorbing present subjects to living men, it is much more so with the spoken drama which men go to hear merely for amusement and pleasure. These dramas of Shakespeare, which are now immortal, might have perished likewise, so far as concerns anything that their author is known to have done for their preservation. We do not find at that period that men bequeathed any literature as personal property ; and as plays were scarcely accounted literature, there was all the less probability of an author bequeathing them.   In Shakespeare's will there is no mention of his plays whatever ; for he had, no doubt, sold them to the theatre and been paid for them. If he had intended them to be published afterwards, his honest, ingenuous and beloved friends, Heminge and Condell who collected them, would certainly have said so, for in their preface to the collected dramas they apologise for publishing them.

Although Shakespeare's parents were probably both septuagenarians, their family was generally not long lived ; but it is very pathetic, in our full knowledge of the immense debt the world owes to this most remarkable man, to think that he should not have lived longer than fifty-two years, to have had some foretaste of the appreciation of mankind for

fine copy, was bought for £300 ; quite perfect copies of all will fetch more. These single plays were probably first sold for 2*d.* or 3*d.* at most.

his life's labour. There is no appearance whatever that he had much indication of this, though the researches of scholars have found over one hundred and fifty "allusions" to Shakespeare in contemporary literature before his death.[1] As to the applause his plays received when acted, this he had fully appraised in his own summing up :—

> Life's but a walking shadow, a poore player
> That struts and frets his houre upon the stage,
> And then is heard no more ; it is a tale
> Told by an ideot, full of sound and fury,
> Signifying nothing.[2]

There could hardly be anything more hopeless when the earth closed on Shakespeare's grave than the expectation that any more would be heard of his unprinted plays, beyond the applause that they might be greeted with when produced at the Globe Theatre, whose property almost, if not entirely they were ; for there were numerous other dramas which were played to suit the public taste for novelty and change, and there is no evidence that his plays would have had any other fate than those dramas, of which most have passed away, forgotten or perished.[3]   But a remarkable concurrence of circumstances caused them to be preserved.

No collection of the plays of any playwright had appeared in England up to the time of Shakespeare's death in 1616.   In

---

[1] See the New Shakspere Society's "Centurie of Praise," and "Further Allusions to Shakspere."   [2] Macbeth, act v., scene 5.

[3] Every search has been made, and there has not been found a single MS. of Shakespeare's, so it has long been concluded that all have perished ; and so extremely rare are original MS. dramas of the period, that there are only very few in the British Museum, and some fragments of others, almost all being by unknown writers.

that same year Ben Jonson, having arranged with the owners
of his dramas, published ten of them in a volume, entitled *The
Workes of Benjamin Jonson.* Such an unusual occurrence
made some stir among the players, who had a laugh at Ben's
expense for calling his plays his " Workes." He also gave
a list of the players who played them, among them we find
Shakespeare, and others of his friends, as Burbage and
Condell. It would be quite natural for the players who knew
the qualities of the dramas better than any, to say " If Ben
Jonson's plays are worth publishing, surely Will Shakespeare's
deserve it more, since not only are they much better, but
there are a great many more of them." Their author was,
however, dead. He would have been the proper person to
arrange with the proprietors of the theatre, as Ben did, and
no one else could be expected to go to the trouble, for the
proprietors of the Globe were not likely to agree to give other
rival theatres their valuable property by publication ; and then,
who was to revise the plays except their author? But in
the course of three or four years, three of Shakespeare's
dearest friends for upwards of twenty years, Dick Burbage,
Jack Hemmings, and Harry Condell became sole owners of
the whole of the sixteen shares into which the proprietary of
the Globe Theatre was divided ; and being well-to-do, it
probably entered into their minds that the world should know
what an able man their Will Shakespeare was. They all wore
mourning rings for him. He left them legacies in his will,
although he had quitted the theatre for three or four years. It
could not be that they expected much, if any, pecuniary gain
by the publication, for Ben Jonson's collection of plays was slow

of sale, and no second edition was called for. The opportunity
had arrived when they could show their esteem for their
departed friend without injuring any interests but their own.
There must have been something about Shakespeare of the
most winning character, that those who knew him well should
speak in such affectionate terms of him, and take so much
trouble to show it. Genius, evidently, had no arrogance in
him, or affectations of superiority. His fellows had no pro-
fessional jealousy, but, as Ben Jonson said, they " loved the
man."

Burbage died in 1619 at fifty-two years of age. We
first hear of Condell in 1598, playing in Ben Jonson's *Every
Man in his Humour.* The tradition of the players was, that
the manuscript of this play had been seen by Shakespeare
when Jonson was in very low water, and had by him been
introduced to the theatre—as well as Ben to the public ; an
act always remembered with gratitude by Jonson. Shakespeare himself took part in the play, and so did Burbage. As
Condell's wife had his shares after his death, he must have
continued his connection with the theatre until the last. His,
and Hemming's name stood at the head of the players in the
patent granted by Charles I. to them in 1625. We know very
little of either of them. The parish books show that they were
respected, by the offices to which they were appointed. This
is saying much, for players were held in low esteem in the
City, which was very puritanic and inveighed strongly against
the stage. We find that Condell played with Burbage in
most of Beaumont and Fletcher's dramas, as doubtless Shakespeare did in their early plays. Condell lived in the parish of

t. Mary, Aldermanbury, London, for upwards of thirty years;
-he was a sidesman in 1606, he had nine children ;—but
as living in the country at Fulham in 1625. In that year
ie plague in the City was very bad in summer and autumn ;
ie theatre was closed as usual in times of plague; and the
ergyman, together with large numbers of parishioners were
irried off by it. Condell died in 1627. All that we have
emaining of him is the signature to his will.

"Old Hemmings," as he was called, though he signed
s name "Heminge," was probably an actor before Shake-
ieare. In his will he describes himself "Citizen and
rocer." He also lived in the parish of St. Mary for forty-
'o years. His business was doubtless managed by his
fe, as was customary. It was unusual for players to
'e far off the theatres. Aldermanbury was a convenient
stance from the " Theatre " at Shoreditch, where they
ted before the theatre was removed to Southwark, after
e "Globe" was built in 1599. Heminge, like Condell, had
een sidesman, and was also trustee of parish property in
io8. He had a family of fourteen children, and died in
i30. Of him we have nothing left, for, unlike Condell,
though his will was drawn up while he was ill, it was not
·en signed, which evidently shows that he died before he
is able to execute it. It was a plague year. Heminge's
ime was at the head of the " King's Players " in 1619,
ondell coming next, Burbage being dead. Heminge took
more personal interest in the finances of the theatre, for his
ime appears as the receiver of payments in the warrants
anted for sums of money for performances before the Court.

LEFT TABLET.

There seems every probability that both Heminge and Condell relinquished the active duties of their profession about the time they undertook the collection of Shakespeare's dramas for the press, as we do not find any trace of them afterwards as players. In 1608 they each had two shares out of twenty in the Blackfriars theatre also.

To these two men, Heminge and Condell, mankind is indebted for that precious volume we now call "Shakespeare."

They, and they alone, by their affection for their departed comrade, undertook the task of collecting and publishing his dramas ; and they modestly apologise for doing what they wished their author had lived to have done himself. They say, in the preface to their book, that they are but "a payre, so carefull to shew their gratitude . . . . to the dead." "We have but collected them and done an office to the dead to procure his Orphanes, Guardians, without ambition of selfe-profit or fame, onely to keepe the memory of so worthie a Friend and Fellow alive as was our SHAKESPEARE." It is impossible to doubt the genuineness of this tribute of affection for their departed friend. It seems probable that Burbage's name would have been associated with them, had he lived, as he was longer with Shakespeare than either Heminge or Condell ; for there is every reason for believing that the whole of the plays were produced with Burbage's knowledge, and he always took the chief parts in them. He was the original Hamlet, Macbeth, Shylock, Richard III., and similar characters. His consent to the publication must have been obtained before his death, for he held so

many shares that his executors might otherwise have reason-
ably objected. He would therefore seem to have died soon
after giving it, for the pair do not name their friend Burbage
as taking part with them in collecting the plays. This seems
to show that they commenced the work of collecting in 1619,
or soon after the death of Burbage. To accomplish this
they had to search through the accumulations of thirty-five
years of play books, and select those they could be sure were
the veritable works of their friend. They, apparently, got
one or two plays from other theatres which they knew were
Shakespeare's. None of the players of that historically cele-
brated company were more competent for the task than
Heminge and Condell, from their long knowledge of Shakespeare, as well as from playing their parts in his dramas with
him, instructed by him, and so much of his best work being
done while they were associated together. They must have
been industrious, careful men. Whatever plays for which he
wrote prologues or epilogues, or that he altered and revised,
they left out of their collection ; their business was to collect
Shakespeare's own complete dramas, and these alone.[1] They
knew them well, for they were among the players who
assembled at the taverns after the play had been returned
from the Master of the Revels—who had the power to alter
or strike out parts—to hear Shakespeare himself read his
own compositions, over their wine, as was customary on a
new play being produced ; and no doubt by the experience of
these practised actors, their quality as acting dramas was

---

[1] They left out *Pericles*, already twice printed in quarto, though much
of the last three acts seems to be by Shakespeare.

RIGHT TABLET.

much improved while being read. They also knew all
the marginal and other alterations, omissions and additions
which had been made to suit the circumstances of rehearsals,
revivals, or the public, together with all the directions on them
—many on inserted scraps of paper—to meet the exigencies
of the time. They well remembered, too, the applause with
which the finest parts, read for the first time, must have been
greeted with by these competent critics. And if Heminge and
Condell are not free from error, it is absolutely certain that they
used their best judgment. It is a pleasure to read their own
statement in their preface that the plays are delivered to the
public "as he conceived them." "Who, as he was a happie
imitator of Nature, was a most gentle expresser of it. His
mind and hand went together. And what he thought, he
uttered with that easinesse that we have scarce received from
him a blot in his papers." Ben Jonson wrote : " The players
often said, in his writing, whatsoever he penned he never
blotted out." This testimony of Heminge and Condell, with
Shakespeare's own handwriting before them, is most valuable.
He was accounted one of the swiftest of the playwrights.
His two friends were not literary men, as their preface indi-
cates, and the form and arrangement in the First Folio seems
to have been arbitrary. They copied Ben Jonson's volume
in giving a list of the players who performed in the plays ;
and this, at the present day, is of great interest and value.

There had been fourteen separate copies of the plays
published in small quarto ; and some of these, before the
authentic editions appeared, had been garbled, and four
others mutilated. It is to such as these that Heminge and

Condell refer in their preface, as "diverse stolne and sur-
reptitious copies maimed and deformed by the frauds and
stealthes of injurious impostors that expos'd them ; even those
are now offer'd to your view, cur'd and perfect of their limbes,
and all the rest absolute in their numbers."[1]

Out of the thirty-six dramas which they published, half
were never printed in any form, and, with the four mutilated
copies named, no less than twenty-two of these great plays
first saw the light in this famous First Folio.   Among these
were such plays as *As You Like It*, *Julius Cæsar*, *King John*,
Macbeth, *The Tempest*, *Henry VI.*, *Measure for Measure*, *The
Taming of the Shrew*, *Twelfth Night*, *The Comedy of Errors*, &c.,
all of which might otherwise have been lost to the world.
Considering then, that whatever of the dramatic literature of
that age has been preserved, has been chiefly kept through
the research of scholars into all Shakespeare's surroundings,
we may fairly conclude that even these would probably all
have disappeared together but for this famous collection of
Heminge and Condell [2] and the name of our great national
poet would have been comparatively little known. The labours
of these two worthies are therefore altogether priceless.

Nor must the enterprise of the printers, who were
the publishers of this collection of dramas, fail to be acknow-
ledged.   On the title page we learn that the book was
" Printed by Isaac Iaggard and Ed. Blount," and on

It is considered certain, from comparing these quartos with the First
Folio of Heminge and Condell, that their statement is not quite applicable to
every quarto.   One or two of them are very correct, and their readings
improved.   [2] See note 1, page 11, and note 3, page 13.

the last page "Printed at the Charges of W. Jaggard, Ed. Blount, I. Smithweeke, and W. Aspley." Whether Heminge and Condell offered the MSS. to the printers, or the printers asked to be permitted to print them, is altogether unknown. It was natural to think that while printers had eagerly seized every opportunity by stealth or otherwise, to print single plays, but were prevented, it would be to their advantage to have the whole, selected by his personal friends, whose property they were. Doubtless the publishers expected to make a legitimate profit by their enterprise. While it is quite clear that Heminge and Condell did not take the risk of publication, it is equally certain that they looked for no profit by it,[1] for they—personal friends of long standing—distinctly state that their only object in what they did was "to keep the memory of so worthy a friend and fellow alive as was their Shakespeare."

The book was published in 1623, in folio, at the price of twenty shillings. Collier says : "The book does credit to the age, even as a specimen of typography." We are not able to say the number of copies that were printed. It was not quick of sale ; a second edition was not called for until nine years afterwards, when Heminge and Condell were both dead. There is the highest degree of probability that the First Folio was produced in the small parish of St. Mary, Aldermanbury ; for wherever the manuscript plays were kept, the collectors would most probably arrange them for publication at their homes, as they lived so near each other. Being such close friends, Shakespeare doubtless often visited them when in London.

[1] Page 17.

Every student cannot but express his gratitude to them for giving us this series of plays by their publication. Collier says he cannot enter as fully as he could wish of " How much we owe to Heminge and Condell." Halliwell-Phillips, who not only gave the largest portion of his life to everything relating to Shakespeare, but a considerable fortune also, says, " If they had not volunteered in affectionate remembrance of their colleague to gather together the works of Shakespeare, some of the noblest monuments of his genius might, and probably would, have been for ever lost."

There is no doubt that the English language as it now is, owes more to two books than to any others, namely, the English Bible and Shakespeare's dramas. The purity and beauty of the English Bible, as Cardinal Newman pathetically said after he left the English Church, " is like the distant bells of an English country church ; the music is always in our ears, and can never be forgotten." But beautiful as the English Bible is, it is limited in its range of language compared with Shakespeare. His plays embrace every variety of thought, wit, humour, eloquence, beauty, majesty, pathos, grandeur, as well as the utmost delicacy of expression, with all that we use in our daily life in writing and speech, expressed in the happiest way possible. Indeed, we are told that in his own day it was said that, " whatever was written well by other men, you would find the same always better expressed by Shakespeare." Happily both Shakespeare and the Bible are the production of the self-same era, independent of each other, so that the English of both is the same, and both have profoundly impressed our language.

Universal testimony has pronounced this Folio of Shakespeare unrivalled. Honest and classic Ben Jonson, in his lines in the prefaces of it "To the memory of my beloved," knew the worth of the precious productions of his friend; and every subsequent age has confirmed all he said, that he was "the wonder of our stage," not even second to the best Greek poets; for he would "call forth Æschylus, Euripides, and Sophocles" to do him honour as "the star of poets." "He was not of an age, but for all time." The book is a standing marvel of one man's work; and the marvel is increased by the fact that such a production should have emanated from that inexperienced young man who first applied for work at the Theatre, Shoreditch, and was, in all probability, glad to take a servant's place. That such depth of thought, delicacy of feeling, wealth of illustration, insight into all human nature, expression, poetry, and eloquence, should have been born of the surroundings that Shakespeare lived in, thrown off in feverish haste to produce novelties for the public, often in the most disturbing circumstances, is a continuing wonder. All poets require time to polish their lines, writing them over and over again, in addition to correcting proofs for the press; but these wonderful dramas were not expected to be printed, or intended for the press, and they never received the correcting hand of the author. It adds to our conviction that they were so, that Heminge and Condell, from their literary inexperience, would be afraid to do anything more than produce the plays as Shakespeare left them for the stage. There probably is no instance of such a mass of superlative

literature from the hands of any one man under such
extraordinary circumstances.[1] Although the plays had
escaped the flames in the burning of the theatre, there still
seemed no hope for them, their author being passed away.
Probably had not Ben Jonson published his "Workes,"
it might never have occurred to Heminge and Condell
that Shakespeare's plays ought to be published also. And
but for the accident of change of proprietorship—the theatre,
whose property they were, falling mainly to these two men—
there could have been no probability of publication. It
was these men's insight into their high quality; it was
their love for their departed friend and his worth, that
made them wish that the world should know his merit also.
It was their unique knowledge of all he did, their self-
sacrifice, their self-imposed labour, when all chance of preservation seemed hopeless, that gave such a precious heritage
as the Folio Shakespeare to all mankind. Every circum-
stance relating to it seems to make it one of the most
marvellous volumes we possess. Happily his friends were able
to do this work before they died, for Condell departed this life
four years after, and Heminge within a further three years.
We can scarcely imagine English literature without
Shakespeare; yet, had it not been for these two unassuming,
modest men—John Heminge and Henry Condell—it seems
inevitable that the world would not have had the Shakespeare it now possesses.

Every English-speaking people has deemed it a duty to

---

[1] The literary matter of Shakespeare's dramas is about equal in quantity
to the whole Bible.

BACK TABLET.

SHAKESPEARE

FIRST FOLIO

Mr WILLIAM
SHAKESPEARES
COMEDIES,
HISTORIES, &
TRAGEDIES.

Published according
to the True
Originall Copies.
LONDON
1623.

We haue but collected
them, and done an
office to the dead; —
without ambition either
of selfe-profit, or fame;
onely to keepe the
memory of so worthy
a Friend, & Fellow aliue,
as was our SHAKESPEARE.
IOHN HEMINGE.
HENRY CONDELL.

ENLARGED FACSIMILE OF FIRST FOLIO ON MONUMENT.

perpetuate the remembrance of our great poet, proving that his friends right nobly "kept the memory of so worthy a friend and fellow alive as was their Shakespeare" by what they did. But it is remarkable that there is absolutely no record or memorial whatever of these two English worthies themselves, except the following two lines, each embedded and hidden among many others in the register of burials of St. Mary, Aldermanbury :—

1627. Dec. 29th.   Mr. Condell.
1630. Oct. 12th.   John Hemmings, player.

This omission is now remedied ; and happily, in doing this justice, we enhance, if it were possible, our estimation of Shakespeare.

A monument is erected to Heminge and Condell in the churchyard of St. Mary the Virgin, Aldermanbury, in the City of London, which is open to the public. In this parish they so long lived, their families were born and brought up ; there they and their wives are buried. It is well seen from the busy thoroughfare. It is of Aberdeen red granite, polished, with an open book of the lightest gray granite representing the famous First Folio ; one leaf has its quaint title page, and on the opposite leaf the exquisite extract from the old players' own preface, already given on page 17.

The four sides of the monument have each a bronze tablet with suitable inscriptions ; and the whole is surmounted by a bust of Shakespeare, also in bronze. The bust is by Mr. C. J. Allen, Professor of Art in University College, Liverpool, and is modelled from the bust of Shake-

speare in Stratford-on-Avon Church (erected by his daughter
and her husband, Dr. Hall, and seen by his widow), and
the portrait by Droeshout in the First Folio of 1623, certified
by Ben Jonson as a good likeness. These are the only
portraits without any flaw in their pedigree; and from
them Mr. Allen has produced a work of art. The granite
monument is erected by Messrs. Alexander Macdonald and
Co., of Aberdeen. The design of the monument and the
inscriptions are by Mr. C. C. Walker, Lilleshall Old Hall,
Shropshire, at whose cost the whole has been produced.
There being no likeness existing of Heminge and Condell,
it was thought more suitable to produce a model of the First
Folio, the publication of which is commemorated. The
tablets speak for themselves. It may be noted that this is
the only public bust of Shakespeare in the City of London.

It is hoped that this memorial of these two English-
men, who deserve the gratitude of mankind, will preserve
their memory to future generations.

www.ingramcontent.com/pod-product-compliance
Lightning Source LLC
Chambersburg PA
CBHW022206020726
47496CB00008B/2906